I0459949

# The Bodies in the Basement
## A Clarke Lantham Mystery

J. Daniel Sawyer

*The Bodies In The Basement*
*A Clarke Lantham Mystery*
by J. Daniel Sawyer

AWP Mystery
A division of ArtisticWhispers Productions, Inc.

Copyright © 2015 J. Daniel Sawyer
All Rights Reserved

Book Design by ArtisticWhispers
Digital painting "Bodies in the Basement" © 2016 Kitty NicIaian

This book is a work of fiction. Names, characters, events, and locations are fictitious or are used fictitiously. Any resemblance to actual persons or events, living or dead, are entirely coincidental.

This file is licensed for private individual entertainment only. The book contained herein constitutes a copyrighted work and may not be reproduced, stored in or introduced into an information retrieval system or transmitted in any form or by any means (electrical, mechanical, photographic, audio recording, or otherwise) for any reason (excepting the uses permitted to the licensee by copyright law under terms of fair use) without the specific written permission of the author.

# Dedication

*Rusch, this is entirely your fault.*
*Thank You*

# THE BODIES IN THE BASEMENT

A CLARKE LANTHAM MYSTERY

J. Daniel Sawyer

11:00 AM, Tuesday

SPRING RAIN, A VANISHING phenomenon in the hills southeast of Oakland in recent years, had hit with a vengeance stern enough to test any basement's drainage system.

At the dead center of Castro Valley, two blocks up from the Village, the basement of the cream-and-maroon, half-assed-villa hand-built plaster house with an orange tile roof remained water-tight, which was just as well, since it was, uncharacteristically, occupied.

Its main floor sat four feet off the ground, leaving just enough room for a ring of windows—two per side—around what would normally be a crawlspace.

In this particular house, it was a partly-finished basement.

The finished part, basically a poured-concrete open-topped box, sank seven feet below the main floor. It took up about a third of the house's footprint, and housed the laundry room and some knockaround couches where the house's inhabitants would retire to read during particularly oven-like weather. It was separated from the rest by a stick-framed sheetrock wall.

A poured path, wide enough to be a hallway, led through an access door to a retaining wall, behind which the rest of the basement consisted of four feet of air and three feet of undisturbed dirt.

This dirt had been a matter of mild irritation for Clarke Lantham, the home's owner, ever since he bought the place—a matter which Nya couldn't help but notice, as he mentioned it every time they happened to be in the basement at the same time.

"It looks like dude got tired halfway through and just gave up," he'd say, every time, looking at the dividing wall as if it were a blight on the landscape. "One of these days..."

And then he'd get on with his laundry.

This afternoon, however, the long-fallow dirt was seeing some serious disturbance.

The two young women, working by lamp light—since the boiling skies outside the half-high basement windows didn't even admit enough light to read by—were covered head to foot in sweat and dirt, and running thin on patience.

What had seemed like a very straightforward job was, they were fast-discovering—a lot bigger than it looked. Digging all of it out was starting to look to both of them like a long way to go to make a grumpy PI feel better about how homey his house was.

"This is your fault, you know," Rachael huffed between spadefuls.

"So not fair," Nya stopped shoveling for a second to clear a stray copper hair out of her mouth, on the grounds that the mud on the end wasn't giving her that minty fresh feeling. "You're the one who said we could do the conversion without him."

"Right, well, about that." Rachael poked at a big clod to break it up. "When I said this was a great idea, you remember?"

Nya didn't look up. Last time she did she'd seen Rachael's face—completely covered in a film of mud except for the bright stripes etched by the rolling beads of sweat and lit from the world's most garish drop-light under her newly restored bright purple A-line haircut (which suited her tons more than the long blonde hair she'd come home with two weeks ago), she'd broken down laughing and inhaled three full clouds of musty basement dirt. She'd rather breathe.

"I think so." Another couple shovels full and

she'd be able to take the next wheelbarrow load up the stairs and out into garden, where the rain made it a hell of a lot cooler than it was down here under all the creosote-smelling heavy oak beams. "You were wearing the top half of your blue bikini and trying to find the bottoms so we could go to the hot tub."

Rachael had also bitched for twenty minutes about the fact that Lantham hadn't put a hot tub in at the office yet, which meant they had to use the condo's tub, which meant no privacy, which meant you had to wear clothes in the water or someone would get butthurt, which was the kind of abomination that the Catholic church *should* be up in arms over, because—unlike people getting married which was a dumb idea no matter *who* did it—shame and stupid-modest bullshit actually had a huge deleterious impact on social health.

Nya felt her cheek twitch up at the memory. Rachael moved like a tornado when she was on a rant, and she had gorgeous round hips, a good fit for the hands, not boxy and flat like Nya's.

Not that Rachael had ever complained about Nya's boxy butt.

Nya continued: "And I said you should go like that—you know you have a cute butt?"

"Yeah, well," Rachael blew a wad of mud-spit out into the dirt. "You can kiss it in all its grimy glory. I don't like Lantham this much. This is a stupid idea. I quit."

She said it. But she kept digging. Mumbling words like "lazy cheap bullshit breakup whining motherfucker."

Clarke Lantham, of Clarke Lantham Investigations, inspired that kind of loyalty. He'd left four days ago to "meet a client" in Dominica.

He actually did have a client. As his secretary, Nya knew that much. But as his roommate, she knew that it wasn't just that. He'd been moping around, dark and heartbroken, for the last two weeks.

He needed the time away. He needed to get laid somewhere. And if he didn't, he was going to be impossible to live with.

But Rachael had a soft spot for Lantham. She wasn't just his junior partner in the business, she carried a torch for him, which she mostly used to set the air on fire when he annoyed her.

Rachael had sworn Nya to secrecy on that point. It was a stupid secret, but Nya had confidence that Rachael's good sense would win out eventually. When it did, she and Clarke would spend a lot less time swearing at each other.

Nya smiled, feeling the pasty mud on her face wrinkle into a ghost mask. "You want to take the next barrow?"

"It's your turn."

"So you want to take the next one?" A little fresh air would keep Rachael's bitching from turning sour.

"Fuck yes." Rachael spiked her shovel into the packed dirt, stepped down over the concrete retaining wall that separated the laundry room from the undeveloped vastness that stretch half-high under the rest of the house. Two hands on the handles, she lifted the barrow.

Nya tossed a last shovel-load on the barrow, kicking up a cloud of dust right in Rachael's face.

"Monkeybrain what the fuck?"

"Sorry." Nya leaned her shovel against a support beam as Rachael trundled the barrow to the staircase and started backing it over the steps.

The foundation footing nearby had a red and a blue Gatorade on it. She didn't care which was which—they all tasted like bland salted lollipops—but Rachael liked the red ones better, so she opened the blue one and drained about half of it.

Thirsty work.

In a day and a half, they'd managed to dig the north half of the basement down about a foot—foot and a half tops. Before they started, they'd done a complete survey of the perimeter, so they'd get a good idea of what they were dealing with.

The front porch of the house was a concrete slab, so it made sense that way in the darkness at the forward end they'd find a cluster of two-by-fours stretching from a hand-poured concrete pier up to the joists supporting the ground floor.

Unlike the rest of the basement, which featured no supports other than the load-bearing piers and cross-joists spaced every four feet running down the center of the house from one end to another, this little area had cross-connected studs every four inches, with a couple exceptions, where remnants of scattered wood bore witness to someone with a hatchet making quick work of a couple of them for access. Probably an afterthought from construction.

It was in there they found their first treasures. A name patch, rank insignia, a medal, dog tags, and some old Army discharge papers belonging to a Master Sergeant Seymore Johanson, who had to be the father or brother of Al Johanson, the guy Clarke had bought the house from.

In the day since, they'd also netted two ancient model kits—a Panzer tank and a British Destroyer, an unopened bottle of vintage root beer, and six vintage and well-worn Matchbox cars.

Nya wondered what they would find next. She was hoping for the wallet of one of the guys who built the house, or some old baseball cards. There were still three feet to go to make the room tall enough for Clarke, then the same amount on the other side of the pier supports. Plenty of chance for more goodies.

Then they had to get some kind of contractor down here to tell them which support walls they could change, so they could knock an archway through and turn the whole area into a rec room. Pool table on one side, movie room on the other.

Rachael was right. They didn't have a prayer of finishing before Clarke got back from his trip on Monday. But that wasn't really the point. He'd been wanting to "finish the house properly," as he put it, since he bought the place, and he hadn't had the time to do it himself or the money to hire anyone else.

After all he'd done for Nya, it was the least she could do. And Rachael—well, Nya figured Rachael just wanted to see the look on Lantham's face.

The water pipes whined. Rachael probably taking a rinse, and wanted more water pressure than the sky was providing. Nya certainly would have if she'd gone out.

No reason she couldn't get the next load piled up and ready.

She grabbed her shovel and used both hands to jackhammer the ground with it, breaking up the hard pack as much as she could.

Shove with the feet, push under the big clods. This one didn't want to come out, but it was okay, they did that sometimes. She kicked at the foot-lip on the spade's rim and broke it loose, then turned the dirt over and tossed it to a spot right near the retaining wall.

It clattered.

"What," she mumbled, "Did I get a rock?"

Nya scrambled over to the retaining wall and looked over. She had to look three times to make sure she was sure she was seeing what she was seeing.

On the bare poured-concrete floor of the laundry room lay a dirty, disintegrating denim rag, wrapped around what looked like a bone maybe nine inches long.

The barrow's wheel thumped light-ish-ly down the stairs.

"Rachael...um...did there used to be a graveyard here?"

"What the...oh my fucking fuck fuck fuck what the hell is this?"

"I don't know, it just came up." Nya pointed at the hole.

Rachael looked a little green.

"Are you okay?"

"Yeah." She backed up, leaned against the post by

the furnace. "I just...hold on." She squatted down. Looked at the bone.

"Is it human?"

Rachael shrugged. "I don't know. It's pretty small. Could be a big dog. Are there any more?"

Nya looked down at the bone. Something deep in her guts slowly twisted. "Don't know. Let's find out."

# 1:00 PM, Tuesday

RACHAEL TOLD NYA THEY would need to be very careful—if it did turn out to be human, they'd need to call the cops in, just in case.

They moved carefully—notwithstanding the efforts of Klepto the dog and Scuttlebutt the cat, who decided to chase one another downstairs and investigate the strange goings on.

It took two hours before they were satisfied that they knew what they were dealing with. They worked with trowels, very carefully, like DIY archaeologists.

They moved six barrows full of dirt, the last of it taken out with trowels, very carefully, until the two smallish scraggly, skeletons, still with patches of hair and leather sticking to them, peaked out above the surrounding dirt of the shallow pit. One male, one female, judging from the remains of wear-ridden jeans and blue and yellow pin-striped button up short sleeve on the one, and chemise tank top and cutoffs on the other.

"No shoes," Nya said as she used a dust whisk to brush the last of the dirt off the female's leg bones. "That's weird, right? Who buries someone with no shoes?"

"Don't touch them," Rachael said from her rest spot on the foundation footings, "The cops'll want to send their lab geeks down.."

"They look like midgets," Nya said, squatting over them.

"No," Rachael's voice shuddered. She crossed her arms protectively over her mud-caked sports bra. "No, they're not midgets."

"So what are they?"

Rachael stared at the grave, as if some kind of answer, more horrible than the bodies themselves, was buried down deeper in the dirt. "I heard about this. In criminal justice class. There was a serial killer here, like, forever ago. The sixties. In Castro Valley. He did kids. Eight of them went missing the same year, there was a big manhunt. They never caught anyone."

"You think that old sweet man Clarke bought the house from was a serial killer?"

Rachael looked at Nya like she was an idiot. "Your Dad killed your three best friends and your boyfriend helped him, and you're surprised that a sweet-talker can do sick shit like this?"

"It's not that, it's..." The last thing she wanted to do was try to explain her fucked-up family to Rachael again. Rachael had all the flexibility of a steel pipe, and no room in her universe for anyone who screwed over their friends or family. And she'd had it easy—two parents, one of them a cop, both of them loved her, both willing to leave her alone whenever she wanted.

So, yeah, sure, she might know all the facts of the case. She might know what Nya's Dad had done to Nya's friends, and to Nya, but she'd never understand why Nya still couldn't hate him. Explaining it again would only make things worse.

"...forget it. It's not important. Look, Twatmonster, if there was a serial killer here, shouldn't we call your Dad? Or the FBI?"

"Yeah, I suppose we...no, wait." Rachael stood up, dug her hand into the thigh pocket on her camo BDUs. She pulled out her phone and started tapping furiously. "They told us in class that it was one of the big unsolved...if we can find the right number, or even better...yes. Twenty thousand dollar reward, still posted. Nya, you know what this means?" Rachael's eyes sparkled in the work lamps.

"That...no." Nya grinned. Rachael started creeping toward her. Their eyes locked, trying to make sure they were each thinking the same thing. "Yes! Oh, shit..."

"The slate-topped table..."

"Those little stools he's always looking at..."

"The beer bar..."

"Yes!" Nya whooped, then covered her mouth with dirt-caked hands when Rachael grabbed her ears. "Sorry."

"Jesus, not so loud."

"Okay, okay. So how do we do this?" Rachael was the one with the police experience, on account of her father being a Sheriff and her getting the criminal justice degree and being Clarke's right hand on all those weird cases for years. Nya mostly knew what Clarke had taught her in the two years she'd been working for him.

"Give me a sec..." Rachael pulled her phone out of her back pocket, tapped the screen a few times. Then she put it to her ear and waited.

"Hey Dad? Yeah, it's me. Fine. Look, you remember that creepazoid up here in CV during the sixties? The Child Culler? Yeah, that one. Well, actually, yeah, I kinda have. What's procedure? Do I call the FBI tip line? AlCo? I mean, if there's still a reward...oh they do. Okay. So...no, it's physical evidence. They'll want to do CSI. Right. No, that's fine, I'll handle it. Thanks. Love you too."

She hung up, stuffed her phone back into her pants and said:

"I'm not talking to the cops looking like I just crawled out of a zombie movie." Rachael looked Nya up and down. "Neither are you. So first: Shower."

THE BATHROOM BETWEEN CLARKE and Nya's bedroom had a glorious yellow tile shower big enough for four—Nya and Rachael fit comfortably.

Nya started with Rachael's back, kneading the bruised muscles while she scrubbed. She figured it was only fair. Rachael was a little taller than Nya—willowy and ripped where Nya was blocky and dwarfish—and no slouch in the fitness department, but the digging and hauling had hurt her lower back and bruises flowered all over her arms and legs where she kept tripping over things while trying to duck the low-ceiling of the dug-out.

While she worked, Rachael said. "The reward is for information leading to the arrest."

"So we'd actually get it this year?" Nya had learned the hard way, working for Clarke, how slow the system moved.

"If we basically solve the case. A case this cold, whoever's got it might just take their sweet time, and we'll hear from them in a few dozen years when the killer confesses in his will or something. Oh god, whatever you're doing, don't stop."

Nya had found a strain under Rachael's right shoulder blade and was rubbing it with her knuckles.

"We can't actually solve it, though," Rachael continued. "We'd be contaminating the case."

"What do you mean we can't solve it?"

"Well, we can't do anything that would disturb the physical evidence, or interfere with the memories of any witnesses we found, or anything. I mean, anything we do, if they do catch this asshole, anything we do could be used by his lawyer to get testimony or evidence thrown out."

"That doesn't sound right. Clarke does it all the time, and there are people that still go to trial."

"Yeah, but he keeps bulletproof...right. *Right.* Okay, okay, yeah, that could work."

"What?"

"Clarke keeps meticulous notes. He records everything. Anything that goes to a prosecutor, he's got the chain of custody on. And he's got it bulletproof. And he never touches any physical evidence—just doesn't get close to it."

"So we pretend we're Clarke? Just do things the way he does them? Do you even know how he does all that?"

"I'd damn well better by now, or he'd have my ass...er...well...you know what I mean. But if the cops jump on this thing, we can't get in their way."

"But if they give it to the lazy cold case guy?"

"Well, there's no law against doing research, right?" Rachael snickered. "Lantham'll be pissed when he finds out we set up a competing operation."

"Hmph." Nya got less mileage out of annoying their boss than Rachael did.

"I'm thinking I'll head to the library, you head to the county recorder's office. We'll find out who lived here way back then, see where he lived, and figure out from there what our next move is."

"Hmm..." Nya squatted down and flicked her open hand across Rachael's butt cheeks.

"You don't approve?"

"I think...you've lived in this neighborhood longer than I have, right?"

"Mmm...about six months longer."

"Squeaker's all squeaky, your turn."

"Squeaker?"

Nya wrapped her teeth around the swell of Rachael's right cheek, right under the little tattoo reading "You Wish" in elegant black script. She bit down, not too hard, but hard enough to elicit a little yelp from Rachael.

"Squeaker." She stood, dangled the loofa over Rachael's shoulder, then turned to have her back scrubbed. "How many of the neighbors do you know really well?"

"Maybe about zero. Why?"

"Because that's the dumb way."

"Bitch." Rachael smacked Nya's ass.

"Ow. Hey!" *So* not fair when they hadn't called play time.

"Don't bitch, bitch. Why's it dumb?"

Nya smirked. It wasn't often she got a leg up on her girlfriend like this. Rachael was *smart* smart, but she looked straight past anything that didn't catch her interest. "Because *some* people get to know their neighbors. Their *old* neighbors."

THEY DECIDED TO SPLIT UP. Rachael would worry about the research—she knew all the databases, and where all the county offices—while Nya hit the pavement.

That was, after she worried about making sure they didn't cut off their own feet by tainting the crime scene.

First thing she did, per her father's instructions, was call the Alameda County Sheriff's Department. They were the only police body with investigative authority in Castro Valley, being an unincorporated township smack in the middle of Alameda County without so much as its own parking enforcement squad. Seventy thousand people crammed into a little bowl in the hills between Hay-weird and Dumb-lin, all of them as inoffensive as a the Mormon Tabernacle choir.

Probably because about half of them actually

were Mormons.

Not a great town for excitement, or even low rents, but it was quiet, had basically no crime, and was the best location in the Bay Area if you were concerned with getting to anywhere else in the Bay Area—just about everything was the same distance away. Silicon Valley, Marin, San Francisco, Livermore, Walnut Creek, all of them were 40 minutes or less if you managed to avoid traffic, and only about three lifetimes if you did something stupid like attempting to put something with four wheels on an interstate between the hours of two and eight pm.

"Do you have a cold case department there?" she asked.

"May I ask what this is regarding?"

"I've discovered something that I think might be connected to an old crime."

"How old?"

"Forty years, maybe."

"Deputy Francisco is definitely the man you want."

"Can I speak to him please?"

"Deputy Francisco isn't in today. Mondays are his day off. If you care to leave a message I can have him give you a call when he comes in tomorrow."

"That would be fantastic, thank you."

"May I inquire about the nature of the

evidence?"

"Bones. Looks like two skeletons. In my basement. Buried under about two feet of dirt." She decided, on-the-fly, that she lived here. She'd find some way to make it stick if it came down to it. Easier than explaining to a receptionist about the whole scheme to build Lantham a rec room while he was on vacation. "Not very tall. I'd guess ten or twelve years old at time of death. I don't remember hearing about there being any old graveyards in this area, and the other stuff around them doesn't look like it's old enough for them to have been buried here before the house was built back in the 40s."

"I see. Will you hold on the line for the forensic examiner?"

"Of course."

She held. For twenty minutes. Her fault for calling in the middle of shift change, at the end of a weekday, but it wasn't like she *asked* to find a pair of skeletons this afternoon.

The forensics guy picked up the phone. Or, technically, the deputy in charge of relations with the forensics labs that the department subcontracted with. In-house forensics were a big no-no—defense attorneys didn't like it when the cops had total control of how scientific tests were done.

Lantham would say "As well they should" and

rattle off a dozen cases where corruption had netted a conviction. Rachael didn't give much of a shit whether a dirtbag went down for drug smuggling, tax evasion, or parking tickets, as long as he wasn't on the street anymore.

*Give it a few years, Rache. You'll see some things that'll change your mind.*

*Fuck off, Lantham.*

She still couldn't quite put her finger on what made him tick. For someone so goddamn heartless his heart sure bled a lot, and in completely useless directions.

She gave the deputy all the same info she'd given the receptionist. She also gave him her name, rank, serial number, and the name of her favorite cat.

Not that she minded. He had the kind of soft, smoked-marshmallow voice that you sometimes heard in black men who'd rasped their throat too much trying to speak below its normal register. A voice like that, she could hang around all day for.

"Look," he said, "You sound like you've got some background in this."

"Criminal justice major."

"Okay, so you probably don't need me to tell you this, but I do have to tell you anyway."

"I'm listening."

"I want you to go downstairs, close the door, and

don't let anyone or anything in there until we can send some people over."

"Already did that. And locked the door."

"Good. Now, I'll have to call around to the labs to figure out who's got CSI available, and then we'll schedule a time to come over and process the scene. I need your phone number and two alternates."

She gave him her number, Nya's number, and the office number.

"Clarke Lantham Investigations?"

"You know it?"

"Your boss has quite a reputation."

"Good or bad?"

"They say he gets results."

"Mmm...suppose that depends on what kind of results you want."

"Thank you, Ms. Oldman. You should be hearing from one of our people in the morning."

SHOULDERING THE NEIGHBORHOOD legwork wasn't a chore for Nya. She'd walked the block, and the two neighboring blocks, almost every day for the past year and a half. She knew every car, every stick of construction, every fleck of paint, and every smell by heart. She'd imprinted it down in her mind like a map of the center of the universe.

Because it was. The center of her universe.

During that time, she'd stopped and talked to almost everybody she'd seen. She figured she'd talked to about three quarters of the neighborhood at one time or another. She'd introduced Lantham around. She was one who first met Teddy Stride and imported him into their lives, with all his interesting adventures.

She was going to miss him. The Stride's house was empty now. They'd left in an awful hurry when they'd been admitted into witness protection. She wondered if she'd ever see him again. He was an annoying kid, but it was the kind of annoying that made the world extra-interesting.

Today, the scent of rain outside was thick enough that she could almost smell how thirsty the ground had been just a few days ago. Long droughts made the whole Bay Area smell tense to her, and the wet, with the pollen bursting out of everything, and the sudden new grasses, it all smelled like relief. The kind of relief she'd felt after surviving a shootout.

She kept getting in the middle of those, and she didn't even carry a gun. Might be worth talking to Clarke about that.

Nya sallied forth in her black-and-pink Any Mountain windbreaker, heading north—and then quickly east—as she rounded the corner on Lorena, aiming for the end unit of the turquoise stucco duplex. The first unit had a garage with no car in the drive. A round, well-fed old man in a denim shirt and raisin-withered papery skin sat on a folding chair beneath the eaves at the mouth of the garage, every day of the year, rain or shine.

He didn't disappoint. She found him just under the shelter of the old single-panel garage door, seated between two TV trays; one with smooth-polished letter openers on the right, and one with blanks cut from deer bone on the left. In his hands was an old rusty pocket knife and one of the blanks, which he was whittling down. When he was done he'd use the three files on the leather mat in his lap to de-burr it and polish it smooth. She'd seen him do it a hundred times before—he always had a good story to tell. Some of them, she figured, might even be true.

She made sure she had the recorder on her phone running.

*Run the recorder, Racahel had said, and make sure you get explicit consent to record on the recording. Don't stop the recording until you leave the conversation. Then load the files up to the server the second you get home. That way we can prove we didn't screw up anybody's testimony. Oh, and don't ask any leading questions.*

"Sugar. You're never round here till five o'clock. How you and your girldyke doing on the big dig?"

"Hiya Smitty! Something came up." Nya walked past him into the junk-strewn garage and retrieved another knife from the old wooden tool table under the broken red wooden kayak hanging from the ceiling, along with a metal folding chair. She opened the chair up and set it down on the other side of his tray full of blanks. "I, uh, forgot I had a paper due. I'm gonna do it on the neighborhood here."

"This old place?"

"Well, it is a bay area landmark."

"Oh, sweetie, you ain't lived."

"Can you tell me about it?"

"You're gonna need some paper, right? I got some around here somewhere..." he started looking around his chair.

"I can just record it..." Nya pulled her phone out, made a show of punching at the dark screen.

"That'll be easier, yeah." Smitty settled back in his chair. Started sizing up the half-finished letter opener in his left paw.

"You and Nan, you've lived here a while, right?"

"Since they built it. Fifty-four. They drummed me out after Korea and then I got on with the union. Helped with the Interstate and all."

"The Interstate?"

"The *Interstate*, sweetie, the *Interstate*. God didn't make 'em, honey. Men did that. Lot of good men died doing it to. We went in there with diggers and cut that channel right through those hills over there," he waved vaguely in the direction of Dublin Canyon. "Buried Cob and Sam and Phil in there when Palomares Hill came down before we could blast it."

"I'm sorry." She laid a hand on his shoulder.

He harrumphed. "They've been dead almost three times longer than you been pissing your diapers, honey. Don't matter now. They can't hear ya."

"Guess so." Nya matched him, whittled as he

whittled. The deer bone shaved off under the knife like ribbons of frozen butter. People answered questions better when you did what they were doing. And if anyone knew who she needed to talk to, he would.

After a few minutes of listening to the rain, she said. "So, my report is, um, well it's on this thing that happened. You remember the Child Culler?"

"Oh, that sonofabitch."

"You know who it was?"

"Nobody knows who it was. He got Adam, though. Little kid from next door. Used to play Cowboys with Curr," his grandson. An electrician. Hunter in his spare time. Nya had met him a few times when he came by to drop off the deer legs Smitty used for his letter openers. "He was a good kid."

"Was anyone else around back then? I mean, anyone who's still living here?"

"Oh, sure, there's loads. Let's see, there was Shirley down at the orcha...no, no she died the year they built that apartment complex over the orchard. Um...hmm...Caputo, he was a good...goddammit, no, he bit it crossing the Boulevard in oh-six. Lewis, now, Lewis over at the Compound, you know that big stone house down by the old library? Corner of Redwood, right down there?" He jerked his head toward the east end of the street. "He was...Jesus H. Fucking Christ. Okay, no." All this time, he hadn't lifted his eyes up from the deer bone in his lap. He normally waved his arms all over the place when he talked. Now he was all shadows and smallness. "Sixty years, honey. Sixty years I been here. Lots of people move on. You'll understand, you know, someday."

"Who all lived around here when it went down?"

"Not a lot. That over there," he waved to the west, across Santa Maria, "That was a chicken farm. Stank like a jungle latrine tank during the summer. That church was there, though. And those two yella houses next...hey, you know, you ever meet that guy Ken over there?"

"The butcher?"

"Yeah. Yeah, that's him. Father was a butcher too. He was here. Was a kid at the time."

"What else was here?"

"Your house. That was here. That dog-ugly house that one Teddy kid lives in. The Hathaways, they were here then too."

"My house—who lived there?"

"Al. You know Al. Sold you the house? Big sweet guy. Probably dead now. Had that tricky heart thing. Oh! Geraldine. Used to own the chicken farm. She's over, that house there." Pointed across Lorena to a ranch home overgrown with magnolia trees and camellia bushes. "You ever met her?"

"No. No, I don't think I even knew anyone really lived there." Someone had to, of course. There was an Explorer in the driveway. But she'd never seen anyone out and about, never seen any lights on.

"She's a morning one. You gotta catch her before noon or she's asleep all night, or in the back shack watching her soaps. Used to have some crazy sex parties over there, back when that was a thing before those queers brought AIDS in and ruined everything." He shrugged. "Guess everything has its time."

"How about you? What do you remember?"

"About the Child Culler?" He pursed his lips, shook his head. "Not a goddamn lot. It was just that one summer. Blazed into town from somewhere. We had eight kids go missing—all three of those kids next door, God that little girl was a sweetie. Used to bring lemonade around in a cigarette tray, selling for a penny a glass, made from that tree you still got there. Yeah, she was a sweet one. Think she was the last to go...or maybe the first? Honestly, honey, it's been so damn long I can't bring it back and I'd be bullshitting if I said any different. Say...you said you need this for school. Aren't you gonna write any of this down?"

"No," Nya smiled. She tapped the cell phone on

her lap. "No, I got it. Just getting background, you know."

"Right, right, you said."

"What about Nan? She had something with her hips..."

And off Smitty was detailing all of Nan's current medical complaints. When that died down enough again, Nya excused herself.

BACK AT HOME, SAFE ON the TV room couch with Scuttlebutt on her shoulder, Klepto on the other end of the couch, her laptop on a tray table in front of her, and a cup of hot chocolate to warm her up from the chilly winter rain, she opened up a new case file.

Date: Today.

Client: It couldn't be her and Rachael, even though they'd found the bones. First off, they were the ones investigating, and it didn't look good in the records because—at least according to Clarke's Rules Of How Things Should Be Done—because the investigator shouldn't have a direct personal stake in the case.

Clarke had started breaking that rule a lot recently, but it wasn't exactly his fault. How was he supposed to know about his Dad, or his best friend, or his brother, or any of those other people who just went lousy when he wasn't looking? At least he knew she understood. And he'd been willing to listen when Nya pointed it out to him, too. That counted for a lot. She needed Clarke to stay Clarke. It was one of those things that bound the universe together. Like duct tape, or the Force. And he was. So she wasn't too worried. Not yet, at least.

Second, even though they found the bones, neither Nya or Rachael had any real vested interest in the case. Sure, it would be fun to figure out who they were and who put them there, and if they caught a serial killer and got a reward in the bargain that wouldn't be a bad thing, but it's not like it was their house. Clarke owned the house, and the dirt underneath it, and he was the one that wouldn't be able to sleep because they creeped him out.

Graveyards creeped him out generally. He didn't seem all that upset by watching people die, but being around them after they'd been dead a while, that was another thing. About the exact opposite of the way Nya felt, but she supposed that's why they made good friends. She could walk him through graveyards, he could hold her when someone got shot.

So, the bones were in the house. The house belonged to Clarke. Nya and Rachael were investigating. Therefore, Clarke was the client.

*Clarke Lantham, homeowner.*

Description of Objective: What did the client want them to achieve? Well, the client, if he was here, would want the dead people gone. He'd also definitely want to know how they got there, and how he got suckered into buying a house with dead people in it. And he'd probably want whoever put those bodies there to get into some serious trouble.

*Identify bodies. Remove from premises. Identify killer. Find and prosecute if possible.*

Yeah, that about covered it.

Billing Terms: She had no idea how do deal with those, so she figured she'd let Clarke work it out. Or maybe she could ask Rachael, or...

Or, if they solved the case and got rid of the dead people, he could put a hot tub in. Or let them put one in with the reward money.

*Client shall furnish firm with one hot tub upon achievement of case objectives.*

Clarke could argue about that when he got home—but that was an argument Nya was pretty sure she could win.

Case Summary: This wasn't the case number—Clarke's system assigned those automatically based on the date and client name. This was more like the one-line pitch for a movie. Something to help the people in the agency remember and refer to the case, shorthand-like.

Nya thought for a moment, then typed *The Bodies In The Basement.*

Now, the notes and files. With the case file created, Nya offloaded the recordings of her conversation with Smitty, and she started transcribing the relevant bits so they'd be available for quick reference.

Rachael wasn't back yet. She'd gone to hit three different county records agencies, and had given up trying to explain why.

As far as Nya could tell, this was a people-story, and if the people were still around, you'd get enough of the story from them to maybe figure out what happened.

She'd already found out, for sure, that the old man Clarke had bought the house from had lived here at the time of the killings. What Nya didn't get was that there was only that summer, when that old man had lived here for all those years. And even though she was the first to admit that she wasn't anything like an expert in serial killers, everything she'd ever seen in a movie, or read in a book, or overheard from Rachael (who studied them extensively) and Lantham (who'd actually caught at least one) seemed to indicate that serial killers didn't just stop. They did what they did because they had some kind of addiction to it.

And Nya understood addiction. Her addiction was one she'd been able to kick, but it took a lot of work and a lot of help. And it took work to get a hold of heroin. Getting a hold of someone to kill, with all the people that ran around the world, that couldn't be very difficult. And she couldn't imagine that if she was addicted to killing people—like she'd been addicted to heroin—she'd ever be able to stop.

 2:00 PM, TUESDAY

*YOU'LL BE HEARING FROM our people in the morning.*

The words rang in Rachael's ears. The kinds of words you only ever hear from people who weren't allowed to say "fuck off" on the telephone.

Here she had physical evidence for one of the biggest unsolved crimes in Bay Area history, and the best they could do was "We'll call you in the morning."

She'd had bum dates more polite than that.

She could just call the FBI. That would get a response. She still had SAC Ronald Rivers's personal cell phone number in the agency files.

Except that she didn't actually know this was connected to the Child Culler. Not in any way she could prove. Those kids had to have been murdered, sure—okay, probably had to have been murdered—but murder wasn't a Federal crime, it was a local one. Hell, serial killing wasn't a Federal crime, locals just got help from the FBI on them because the FBI had a whole department for dealing with serial killers, since serial killers so often crossed state lines.

Which was why her first stop was going to be the offices of the Oakland Tribune. If anyone was going to have electronic records of all the old newspaper reports from the area, the Trib offices would. They weren't the local paper for Castro Valley back then, but the Child Culler was national news, and Oakland was the nearest real city, and had been a real city even way back then.

Just to be sure she needed to take the trip, she tried Wikipedia. Glorious oracle of all things trivial and interesting though it was, it did not have a good article on the Child Culler. With killers like Doodler, Warner, Alcalla, Zodiac, and Bundy competing for attention in the late sixties and early seventies, a flash-in-the-pan three month disappearance spree didn't stand a chance of sticking in the public imagination. Not even with a snappy name like "Child Culler"—because, up until today, there hadn't ever been any proof that any of the kids who disappeared were murdered.

*If* this was a Child Culler crime. *If.*

The twentieth century, after all, with its permeable travel paths, easy-to-forge documents, and easy smuggling paths. And the middle of the twentieth century? Well, there had been a lot of places where kids could get sold off to wealthy expatriates. That kind of thing had happened before. The two kids in that basement could have nothing whatsoever to do with the disappearances. Or someone might have used the Child Culler's antics as a cover for some other sick game.

It was all hypothetical at this point. All of it.

Rachael had to keep reminding herself of that as she threaded her way between lanes of traffic on her Suzuki Ninja.

If Lantham had taught her nothing else, it was that if you limited your questions too soon, you risked fingering the wrong culprit, and letting the right one go free.

Her Dad used to talk about that too, back when she first got into college going after her criminal justice degree.

And she'd seen it first-hand, too. A couple times now.

Had to keep that in mind.

But whoever the bastard was who killed those kids, he was going down. Even if she had to dig up his grave to do it.

On 880 North at mid-day on a Tuesday, the traffic generally flows like blood through atheroscleurotic veins. It's fine, it'll go where it needs to in a reasonable amount of time. But if anyone so much as sneezes at the wrong time, the whole goddamn system could come right to a standstill.

Today was a typical Tuesday, so Rachael made good time heading out to Oakland, even though the further she got, the less the traffic resembled fast-flowing blood and the more it resembled cold-weather treacle.

She exited at Hegenberger, turned left and followed the road west over the overpass, then turned right onto Oakport Road.

The Trib's offices were in the Zebra building.

That wasn't its official name, but it should have been. A twelve-story office complex across the freeway from the Coliseum, it alternated black windows and white tile all the way up to its roof-line, like the architect had designed it while looking at a goth-girl's stripey socks.

Goth-girl stripey socks were a subject on which Rachael was an acknowledged expert with years of experience—she was wearing a pair under her biking boots as she rolled up on the sidewalk, around the card-access security gate, and parked in an out-of-the-way corner between two unoccupied handicap parking slots.

The Trib was up on the ninth floor. They didn't,

it turned out, actually have any digital archives going back that far. Best they could do was microfische. But if she was willing to search through those, they'd be happy to set her up with a reader.

But wasn't there any easier way?

Well, the secretary had heard some rumblings about a project up at UC Berkeley trying to digitize all the local papers for their school of journalism. That might be a good place to start.

It was, Rachael had to admit to herself, better than nothing. And the extra time on the road helped bring her down a bit.

The day had keyed her up way more than she wanted to admit. She was an adult human being, she'd seen a murder scene or two—hell, she'd seen an actual murder or two—and it's not like anything any sick fuck did surprised her. If anything, sick fucks were frustrating because they were *so* predictable. Every time she ran into a new one—a new serial killer, especially—some small part of her, the part that loved scare stories around the campfire, hoped to God there would be something that would really shock her down to her socks.

Shock was fun. Kind of reminded you that you were alive—and that you cared about it.

And besides, there were certain kinds of douchebaggery that deserved props just for the sheer twisted genius.

But sitting right up there where the apex of twisted genius should be—the ones that had to hunt humans to get their kicks—things got...well, *predictable* after a while. Either they were blood freaks, or they were sex freaks—and not the fun kind—or they ate or fucked whoever they killed. Or, sometimes, they were just bored and didn't really care if anyone found out anyway.

The real Hannibal Lecter types? They never really showed up.

Okay, once in a blue moon.

And there were some real scary types, really good for horror movies.

But not many of them.

Most of them were just used car dealers who kept women in freezers or hung their bodies to dry in the shed or made guys they picked up at clubs drink drain cleaner before burying them in the backyard. Boring shit

Not boring for the victims, sure. Terrifying for the victims. Petrifying. But not exactly breaking new ground in the creativity department. And that pissed Rachael off.

Not that anyone should *aspire* to serial killer-hood, or that serial killers ought to actually have, you know, any freedom to pursue their little fetishes. But really, if you're gonna do something seriously fucked up, you owe it to your own basic dignity to show a modicum of creativity and style.

Doing something as desperately fucked up as killing people for fun *ought* to be an opportunity for some kind of expressionism. Individuality. Flare, even. At least, to Rachael's way of thinking.

But even here, with the Child Culler, was there any kind of panache? Not as far as she could see. All she could see were bodies in the basement. Gacey already did that one in a big way. Okay, so Gacey came later, but he wasn't copycatting the Culler. It's not like he could have copied a killer that got no press at all, right?

There was, Rachael decided as she got off 24 before the tunnel, an essential lameness about most serial killers that you couldn't get away from. Rent-a-cop lameness. Blonde-joke lameness. Star Wars prequel lameness.

But she'd wanted to bag one ever since she'd learned about them. Lantham's takedown of the Broadway Slasher was what put him on her map. It's why she got onto a law enforcement track. And it's why she wound up working for Lantham, which made her give up on ever being a cop.

But she never gave up on bagging a serial. And, now that she was face-to-face with it, she couldn't figure out why.

Sure, it was sexy, taking down someone that awful. But, now that she thought about it, she wondered if it was their lameness that made them look like a brass ring to her. If she was honest with herself, she had to admit that most crime was, essentially, boring. There were only so many ways to rip something off, kill someone, rape someone, or cover something up. The challenge with serial killers was finding them.

They were the wolves in sheep's clothing. The sharks in the surf. The snakes in the grass. The clichéd threat in the obligatorily glib setting description. Killers that looked just like everybody else, except they occasionally made people disappear in ways that you usually didn't see this side of a medieval battlefield. And you could look right at them, talk right to them, and never know they were the droids you were looking for.

If there was one thing she hated more than anything else in the world, it was people that lied about who they were. Trapped other people. Lied to them about what they wanted. Lied to themselves. Covered it up afterwards.

And maybe if she could put enough fuckers like that away...

Well, then maybe the world would suck just a

little bit less.

She had to hunt around a little bit to find the right archives, then she had to pretend she lost her student ID and bat her eyelashes at the cute work-study student behind the counter, but when she mentioned she was doing a paper on the coverage of an old serial killer case, it was like she'd said the magic word.

Maybe the whole world just loved a good serial killer.

Almost as much as the old papers loved a good abduction.

4:30 PM, TUESDAY

THE RAIN GOT WORSE AS the afternoon went on. When she was done transcribing, Nya left her computer in the TV room and went to the front door to check the mail.

Standing by the front windows, looking out through the warbly pre-war plate glass at the long-overdue storm turning Santa Maria Avenue into a river with an asphalt sandbar in the middle of it. It didn't make a dent in anything else that might be buried down below, but it was nice to think that somehow it made the place clean.

Rachael was the one who knew about this killer in the first place. She knew things about serial killers in general. Nya kept her eyes on the water outside while she dialed the number two speed-dial on her phone.

"Monkeybrain!" Rachael's customary phone greeting when she saw Nya on the caller ID.

"Twatmonster!"

"What did you find out?"

"Nothing we didn't know, I don't think. But I was wondering. You know about serial killers and stuff?"

"Are you kidding? I had a poster of Ted Bundy on my bedroom wall in high school."

"Who's that?"

"Trust me, sweetie, you don't want to know."

"Well, do they just, like, stop?"

"Stop what? Killing?"

"Yeah. I mean, this Culler guy. He did eight kids, but it was only the one summer."

"Far as I know."

"But those two bodies, they're here in the basement, and that old man, he was here for sixty, seventy years, right?"

"Something like that, yeah."

"And...well, you said they haven't caught this Culler guy, but you also said he was only around way back then. Did he kill anyone else anywhere else? Do they know?"

"I haven't found anything yet. At least, not in California." Rachael rustled on the other end of the phone, then mumbled "Check...out of state...abduction...got it. Why?"

"So, do they just stop?"

"I...I don't know. I don't think so. There was this

one book...Fallon, I think...said it's like taking a shit. You can control when you do it, but not the fact that it'll happen."

"So why were there..."

"...only eight?"

"Exactly."

Rachael hmm'd for a moment, then said: "Maybe the guy that sold Lantham the house..."

"Al."

"Right. Maybe Al didn't do it. Maybe he had a visitor."

IT WAS WORTH LOOKING INTO. That's what Nya did for the rest of the day. Umbrella in one hand, phone in her pocket set to record, and a purse full of candies stolen from the earthquake cupboard downstairs, she toured the neighborhood in search of senior citizens.

She felt kind of like she was playing hide-and-seek, which she hadn't done in years.

First stop was Geraldine, Smitty's across-the-street neighbor, who Nya had never actually met. Everyone else, who looked like she wasn't home.

No answer at the door.

Sneaking down the driveway, past the Explorer—which had a coating of dust on its windshield that must've taken at least three weeks to accumulate—and through a rickety mossy rounded-slat side gate, Nya found a building in the back behind a ten foot hedge of junipers. It looked a lot like the setup at Clarke's house, with the detached garage having been turned into a whole separate unit. A guest house, in this case, instead of the office for a detective agency.

The door was painted green—or had been a long time ago. And there were three frosted windows in it at head hight.

And it was standing open.

There was a woman inside. Older-verging-on-old. Maybe sixty-five or seventy. Kinda dumpy, but not a slug, with rainbow hair and silver roots. She was slouched on a cushy canvas sofa looking at a television, more-or-less facing Nya.

She didn't smell right. And it wasn't because she was blasted out of her mind on Grey Goose and some little red pills. Nya could smell those each on their own. Blood alcohol about twice the driving limit. Enough secobarbital to make even Lantham mellow out for two days straight. Nya's friend Stephanie used to like seccies. Nya couldn't stand them herself. All the down-and-drowsy of heroin, with none of the joyful hunger-slaking full-body braingasms. It was like eating bacon fat without the bacon part.

Between the alcohol and the seccies and the two-days unshowered post-menopausal body odor, there was another thread. Something...something she'd only smelled before in people who weren't quite right in the head. Maybe it was a hormone, or a lack of some neurotransmitter, or some protein that wasn't in the right balance. Clarke was into that kind of stuff, he'd come up with some theory. Nya didn't know enough about the science of what her nose did to lay a clear finger on it. All she knew was that the woman on the couch smelled like she was lost.

"Geraldine?" Nya knocked on the door. "Hello?"

"Hmm?" The lazy pale blue eyes flitted from the screen to the door. "Oh, hi, honey, come on in, come on in. I didn't think you'd be around here today. How are you, darlin'?"

It sounded like she was talking through a mouthful of cotton. It wasn't a relaxed kind of slow slur. More like listening to newscaster speak in slow motion. Nya found herself hanging on every word, waiting for the next one, and fighting an adrenaline surge when it didn't come fast enough.

"I...uh...we've never met."

"Oh? But we have. Haven't we? Cindy! What are you doing here?"

"My name is Nya..."

"No, no..."

"I'm a friend of Smitty's."

"Oh. Smitty." She smiled. Her teeth looked like she'd done a little too much meth over the years. "Smitty. Well, come in. Sit down. Have a drink?"

Nya went in. She explained how she was doing a college report on local history and asked if she could record things. Geraldine forgot about it less than a minute later, and started talking to Nya as if Nya were her daughter.

It made her blood rise. She was still getting used to not having a mother, and nothing about this woman seemed at all maternal—well, aside from the way she turned nasty when Nya made any move to get away.

The candies helped. Nya figured she'd like the chocolate since, in Nya's experience, all old ladies loved chocolate. Geraldine ignored the Lindor truffles though, when she saw the gold foil wrapping on the Werther's originals.

They didn't help her focus, though. Nya spent an hour trying to wring some sense out of Geraldine, but anytime she came around to mentioning the killings, the old woman started crying and telling her to get the hell out, until Nya reached the doorway, when Geraldine called her back and begged her not to go, because she never got to talk to anyone except sometimes on weekends when she made it out to church. And because Nya reminded her of her daughter. One of the girls that disappeared.

"You know, those hot days? The sweat days? The days little girls go out in sun dresses with African Daisies in their hair? Every time we have a day like that, I think, maybe today Annabelle will come in, with a little purple daisy in her hair, wanting to know if she could go over to Nina's to play in the sprinklers..."

Nya felt as if someone had shoved an icicle through her breastbone. There were, she knew first hand, some people who never left. Good or bad, loved or hated, no matter how dead they were or how long they'd been that way, they were always lurking just outside the door, waiting to knock.

## 5:42 PM, TUESDAY

GERALDINE PASSED OUT AFTER a while, which gave Nya a chance to finally leave.

It was edging towards dark outside—the sunset peeking through the occasional cloud break in flashes. Winks in the gray, fleeting sparkles of color, like a four-year old hiding in a closet.

She headed back to the home soil—or home mud river—of Santa Maria, and headed south through the bucketing rain, past the house, then across the street-stream to the old clapboard yellow Craftsman that housed Ken the butcher and his family.

She knocked on the peeling white wood-framed screen door.

A five year old boy dressed in cutoffs, goosebumps, and nothing else answered the door.

"Nya?"

"Hey Clint. Is your..." The fact that he was dressed for a summer heat wave brought her up short. "Hey, aren't you a little cold?"

"Me? Nah." He smacked himself on the chest. "I'm a real man, I can take it."

Five seemed awfully young for he-man bravado. Then again, Nya didn't have any brothers, so what did she know? "Is Ken home?"

"No. Daddy's down at work." His adopted father. Ken and Celia had given up on having a new kid on Celia's fiftieth birthday, three years ago, and gone shopping for a used one. They did a good job. He was a sweetheart—so were Ken and Celia. Good neighbors, like most people around here.

"Do you know when he'll be back?"

"He's working till after my bed time tonight." Damn it. "But he's got tomorrow off. We're going up to Discovery Kingdom and he said we could get cotton candy and…"

"Clint?" A woman's cigarette-rasp came from the back room. That would be Celia. "Who is it?"

"It's Nya, Mom."

"Well, shit, go on and send her in."

"Come on in," the boy unlatched the door, shrugged, and returned to the cracked leather lay-z-boy, where he picked up an iPad and proceeded to do whatever he'd been doing before he heard Nya climbing the porch steps.

The house had the classic Craftsman layout that

Clarke talked about all the time—two main rooms, a living room and a dining room, separated by a notional half-high wall that only came about halfway across the dividing space between the two. Crown molding, lath and plaster walls (chipped and coming down in spots) stained and unvarnished hardwood floors that were about thirty years overdue for a waxing. The door frame leading into the hallway had pencil hashes and name scrawls on it, where the Baxters had measured their children and charted their growth for two generations now.

"So what's his deal with the no-shirt in the..." Nya turned the corner at the back of the living/dining room and found Celia in the kitchen, the windows open, the dishwasher running, scrubbing a load of pots in her yellow dish gloves and smoking a Marlboro menthol while she listened to Led Zeppelin on the radio. "Oh. I'm sorry, I didn't mean to..."

"Nonsense, relax." Celia kept scrubbing, her blond braid popping in time to the hard bass riffs in Kashmir. "Clint's got an initiation. He has to spend all day from school to bedtime shirtless, with no blanket, and stay on video chat with his 'commander' to prove it, or he loses his—oh, how'd he put it—'claim to a prime place in the world's most exclusive top secret club.'"

"Sounds weird."

"It's boys. My brothers were the same way. So I gave up trying to get him to put on a sweater. Let him freeze if he wants to. Want a beer?"

"Sure."

"Fridge."

Nya crossed behind her to the clamp-handled Kenmore by the laundry room door. She yanked it open—which took a non-trivial amount of heft—and surveyed the selection of Miller Light, PBR, and, mercifully, a Pyramid IPA.

"Okay if I grab the IPA?"

"Please. Can't stand the stuff. Ken's brother brings it over cause he thinks beer should be classy."

"Thanks." Nya hooked her fingers around the neck, rescued the bottle from the fridge, opened it with the opener that was stuck to the fridge with a floral ceramic magnet. Since she couldn't get to the garbage—which lived under the sink which Celia was currently using to scour some hard carbon off a cast-iron skillet—she pocketed the top.

The IPA tasted like sharp sunshine. Just the thing for a rainy winter day.

"Not half bad. You should try it."

"Eh. All hops." Celia bounced twice in place. "See? I got enough in me already."

Nya chuckled.

"What brings you over here in this deluge? Figured you'd be building an ark in that back yard of yours."

"I just had to ask Ken something about the neighborhood. Rachael's got this thing for her class, and I promised to help her with her homework, so…"

"She got you doing her research, eh? What on?"

Nya took her phone out. "Mind if I record? Then Rachael can take her own notes."

"Sure, knock yourself out. Just don't put me on the Internet. Never would hear the end of it from my fucking sister."

"Promise."

"Great. So this thing for Rachael?"

"Well, I needed to talk to Ken, really. Smitty said he lived here back in the sixties."

"We both did."

"Really?"

"Met in elementary school. He stole my Hershey bar at lunch and I punched him out. Love at first blood."

"Where'd you live?"

"That duplex where Smitty's living now. Other unit."

"He said some kid named Adam lived there."

"That was my brother." Her voice was a little softer. "He and Smitty's grandson had some kind of secret spy ring going on, keeping the Russians out of town. They were out trying to catch spies every day after school until..."

"Smitty said he disappeared that one summer..."

"When everyone else did, yeah."

"That's what Rachael's paper is about. She's trying to get an idea of what happened to the town. You know how all the serial killer stories are about the killer, well she's doing a thing on the victims and what happened to their community and everything."

"Fucked us up, that's what it did." Celia took a deep drag on the menthol, then turned around so she was facing Nya. "Most things, you know, they happen and they're gone. Then some things happen, and the world stops around you." As she talked, whisps of smoke snaked out of her mouth, and she sniffed them up her nose. "You're never quite you again. I don't think I was really a kid after Joey disappeared. And then Adam..." Celia pressed her lips together, hard, and exhaled the remaining smoke in two great gouts from her nose.

Then she took another drag.

"It made life stop for my parents. It never un-stopped. There wasn't anything like childhood after that."

Despite the cold, a bead of sweat rolled down Nya's spine. "No childhood?"

"Before that summer, we got to go anywhere we wanted, do anything we wanted, but afterwards we had to stay inside to play, we couldn't go visiting any friends without an adult taking us. And did it do any good?"

Nya shrugged. "I don't know, did it?"

"Nope." Her voice had fallen to barely a whisper. Nya hoped the phone picked it up okay. "He kept right on taking us until he wanted to stop, I guess."

"God, how do could you even...with Clint? Aren't you worried all the time?"

"Sure." Celia shrugged and turned back to the dishes. "But that's my job. I'm not going to put him through what I went through. Anyway, after that, not a lot can scare you." She looked into the dark over-sink window. With the light in the kitchen, it made a mirror, where she met Nya's eyes. "And the house you were in, that was the worst."

"How was it the worst?"

"The first kid and the last kid were both taken from that house. Even with Al and Jenny there. Even with Al's brother over for the summer come back from Vietnam.  All those adults around, and the bastard took them right out of the back yard, nobody ever heard from them again."

Nya tried to keep her breathing calm. "And nobody saw him?"

"Nobody. It was like there was this ghost, and it was always around. You wondered what bush he was hiding in, what tree he was up."

Nya's phone rang. Rachael. "Sorry, I gotta get this..."

"Be my guest."

Nya ducked out the back door. "Hey Twatmonster, what's up?"

"It's Seymore."

"Al's brother?"

"Yeah. Fucker came into town for Al's wedding that spring, two weeks before everything starts. I found the article in The Forum about the wedding. He was a big deal here back then, I guess. Anyway, it says the wedding is in May, and then the whole family moves in after the wedding—I said it was her second, right? She had a couple kids. War widow. He had a couple kids too, and their mom was dead and, well, anyway, get this. Two weeks *two weeks* later, the first kid goes missing. it's Al's kid. His younger one, the daughter, while the older one, the boy, he's off at summer camp. Then, six weeks later, both his step-kids. Then the brother blows town."

"Well we have to find him."

"Mmm...and find out if there were more victims wherever he moved..."

6:10 PM, TUESDAY

ONE DISADVANTAGE OF MOTORCYCLE travel: It made working on the road nearly impossible. Her helmet was quiet enough she could talk on the phone if a call came in, but actually using the phone like a civilized multitasker was pretty much impossible.

Which wasn't something that occurred to her until she was halfway down highway 13, rocketing twenty-five miles an hour between lines of cars bunched up like they were waiting for a chance to ride the Indiana Jones Adventure.

*Next step, next step, what's the next step.*

She deliberately resisted asking herself "What would Lantham do?" She already knew the answer. He'd call Earl Whitaker.

Earl would find all the information in the world on Al's brother, and deliver it straight to Lantham's inbox along with his invoice, and Lantham would spend the next week sorting through all of it and figure out some sideways angle to locate the brother, track him down, and confirm his suspicions without ever alerting the target.

That wasn't something she could do. She didn't have a week to spend sorting through the records of someone's life, for one thing. She didn't have the money, either. Earl was the best black market data miner in the country, and he invoiced like it.

And, for another thing, the notion of going in sideways so the target didn't know he was under suspicion seemed...underhanded. She knew there were times when it was the right thing to do—when you didn't want to screw up a trail of evidence, for example, or when you didn't want to ruin someone's day on a bum hunch. Doctor Beschoff, her favorite criminology professor, told her that her problem was a difficulty in separating personal ethics from professional ethics, and that it was something she'd get over—but it really wasn't something she wanted to get over.

If Lantham was here, and did that, she'd harangue him for it, then go along with it, because it was his detective agency, and his call to make. But this was her case. Her responsibility. She was playing lead dog on this one, and...

No. She didn't want to feel that slimy today.

Or any other day.

So how the hell was she going to find Master

Sergeant Seymour Johanson.

Well, she did have the Internet, and by the time she got to Redwood Road she was ready to give up on the rain-and-car-clogged freeway as a bad idea anyway.

Where Redwood crossed 13, just on the uphill side, there was a shopping center that looked like it had sprouted from the ground back in the 1960s when nobody was sober enough to tell "futuristic" from "fucking awful." The Safeway had an arching, sloping roof like it had grown up in Tomorrowland. It was flanked by a two-story squat building that looked like some giant had misplaced his apple crates, and then someone else had come along and painted them gray-blue so that, if they'd been built on a ridge backing up to the sky, they'd blend in perfectly and be safe from shoppers and shoplifters alike.

Except that they were built into the side of a mountain populated by redwoods, eucalyptus, and social climbers.

At the corner where the apple-crates met the swoopy-arch, there was a kind of cave area pretending to be an atrium, complete with fake trees and some slat-benches for smoking on, back when people were allowed to smoke that close to store entrances. Behind the atrium there was a sliding glass door leading into the world's least-well-advertised Walgreens.

The atrium offered enough shelter for what Rachael needed. She popped through into the Walgreens and bought a stylus so she wouldn't have to freeze her fingers off, then sat down on the used-to-be smoking benches.

"Okay, Seymour. Where did you get to?" She connected to the company server, and used one of the people-finder services that the office was always connected to.

A lot of Seymour Johnsons—but not a lot of Seymour Johansons. Also not a lot listing military records. Rachael started clicking through, seeing if any of them were about the right age and looked like they could be Al's brother.

There was one in Whitesboro New York that looked promising, but she wasn't sure that a retired Master Sergeant who was almost seventy would be all that interested in a local indie band named "Three-Finger Shocker."

How the hell were you supposed to find someone on these things anyway? Without a social security number? Lantham could work magic with these databases, but information was useless unless you knew what to do with it. Information without a framework was just data, and data wasn't much better than noise, when you got right down to it.

*You're doing it wrong, Rachael, she told herself. Forget looking clever. This is just a regular crime. This needs basic police work. You've done it before. You know what to do.*

When you've got a suspect, and you can't find him, what's the first thing you do?

You ask his family if they've seen him.

She could look Al up. He'd been a good neighbor. If she remembered right, he'd retired to Capitola...or, at least, somewhere on the coast. He'd talked often enough about watching the sun set over the ocean every night.

Not a happy shiny thought, rousting him. She really didn't want to upset him. He didn't deserve that, not after everything he'd been through. Not after sticking with the neighborhood for all those years, helping start gardens, keeping the neighborhood kids entertained by letting them play in his back yard when the traffic was too thick.

But, deep down, she couldn't believe he hadn't noticed anything weird about his brother. How could you *not* notice anything weird? Okay, so Anne Rule hadn't noticed anything about Bundy, but she should have. Even she admitted that. And she was only his friend, not his sister.

Al was Seymour's brother. Al should have noticed *something*.

Sure, she liked him. She hated the thought of bothering him.

But not as much as she hated the thought of letting his brother get away with murder.

6:30 PM, Tuesday

BACK AT HOME, NYA had decided on her own that the simplest way to find Seymour Johanson was by asking his brother. It hadn't taken her long to find Al Johanson's contact info. Clarke had made friends with him, so they'd kept in touch. Just emails. Every once in a while Clarke had a question about the house, and Al would answer with stories upon stories—two lifetimes worth, at least.

In the emails, he talked about where he'd moved. He had a "lovely little hovel" (his description) on the bluff up on the North Coast; a little town called Bolinas.

Nya hadn't ever been up that far. She'd gone with Rachael up to the nude beach just south of Stinson a few times, but Bolinas was further up, and at the south end of the little subcontinent that was famous for the Point Reyes lighthouse on its western tip.

And, even better, she found Al's phone number—so she called him up.

She hadn't met him, but he remembered Rachael, and he definitely knew who Clarke was, so he was happy to chat with her from outside on his patio, where he was watching the meteor shower when the clouds parted enough for him to see it. He was happy to hear from her, and glad that the house was still in good hands, and was there a reason she called?

She realized that she'd called without much of a script, and now that she was talking to him she didn't think it was a good idea mention that she and Rachael had found bodies in the basement, so she decided to ask him to tell her about how the house had come to be built in the first place.

"Oh, that's a long story. Too long to go into over the phone. Maybe someday I'll come down to check out the old place, and give you a hands-on tour."

"Actually," Nya found herself saying, "Me and Rachael were doing some remodel work, and we found some old things I think belong to you. I was wondering...I'd love to hear that story. What if we brought the things up to you?"

"When were you thinking?"

"That meteor shower sounds beautiful..."

"You are a sweet sweet young woman. I'd love to have you. Just don't make it too late. I turn into a pumpkin after eleven."

RACHAEL GOT BACK A little after seven,

after taking back roads to avoid the atrocious rush hour traffic.

When Nya said the word "Bolinas," Rachael just about blew a gasket.

"You're telling me I have to wade up through that ribbon of shit?"

"No. We'll have dinner first and then go up. I called him, he's expecting us around nine thirty. Asked us to come late so we could see the best part of the meteor shower."

"I am *not* eating dinner in this death house."

"For fuck's sake, Rache, it's only a couple skeletons."

"A couple? *All* of them could be down there. This place is a graveyard of kids, little kids, who were god-knows-whatted to death down there."

"Forty years ago. It's not like they're gonna come up and strangle us while we eat."

Rachael just shuddered. "We'll eat on the way."

"You've been watching too many of Clarke's zombie movies."

"Fuck him. Let's go."

It wasn't normally in Nya's nature to needle, but Rachael was skeeved in a way Nya'd never seen her skeeved before. If she was honest with herself—and she had to be since people so seldom were and she needed to be able to trust *somebody* besides Clarke and

Rachael—she kind of enjoyed it.

But by the time they crossed the San Rafael Bridge, she was wishing she hadn't. Rachael's normally-robust sense of humor was on a starvation diet. For the last twenty miles snaking through the Marin hill country, Nya felt like she was sitting next to a Rachael-shaped block of ice.

It was slow going in the rain, but when they crested the coastal mountains they broke through into the dry, beneath a low and angry sky reflecting the spare red light from the scattered coastal villages, with a band of purple-black stretching across the horizon where the sunset slipped in under the overcast.

Bolinas, across the lagoon from Stinson Beach, wasn't a town that they'd have been able to find without GPS. There was no sign for it on the highway—according to Wikipedia, this was because the locals took it down anytime it was put up. They also meticulously failed to groom the verge along the highway, so the only two turnouts that lead into town were nearly invisible unless you knew what you were looking for.

Doubly so in the dark.

They found the turnout after missing it twice, and wound their way through the thick coastal greenery into the scattered farms and arts-and-crafts shops on the outskirts.

"Turn left at the T-intersection, then right at the stop sign," Nya said. "He said he's up on the plateau, whatever that means. There, right there..."

"Christ, Nya, I see it, okay? It's a T-junction. The road *stops*. Jesus."

"I'm sorry, Rache."

"Forget it." Rachael braked, hooked a right, rolled through the stop sign and snaked up the next hill through a stand of eucalyptus. "I just...don't handle dead things very well."

"But you and Clarke had that murder in Berkeley..."

"And I was a wreck for a month after..."

"And then there was that thing in Weed with Clarke's dad and that biker guy..."

"That was different, okay? Just shut up. This one's bad. I mean...fuck, even I don't know what I mean. But I don't want to do this. There's some things you just don't want to find out."

"So why are we going?"

"Because...because we need this."

"We?"

Rachael didn't answer for a moment. Then she said: "What's my next turn?"

Nya looked at the moving blue dot on her phone. "Evergreen. Left. Just past the fire station."

"Got it."

"So. We?" Nya asked again.

"It has to...I can't let...oh, fuck, just drop it, okay?

Nya laid her hand on Rachael's knee. "You want to...oh." Rachael wanted to take down a serial killer, so she didn't feel like she had something to prove when she and Clarke worked together. Obvious as daylight. "Sweetie, you're not going to make this thing with Clarke any better by..."

"No. No. That's not it at all. Now leave it alone? Please?"

"Okay." Fat lot of good it would do. "But you really should talk to him. It won't get better till you do. Till you know for sure, you know, one way or another."

"Nya, for fuck's sake..."

"Okay, okay," Nya yanked her hands up into 'don't shoot' position. "Fine. I'll shut up."

"And when we get there, better let me do the talking."

Nya tried not to snort out loud. She hadn't seen Rachael actually interrogate anyone, but Rachael didn't do well with things she held in contempt. If Nya didn't manage to get the lead on this, Rachael was like as not to insult the sweet old man before they could find out where his brother was.

Another couple turns, and:

"Just in here, I think." Nya pointed at a little gravel-paved alleyway called Juniper Drive. The street went all the way to the cliff looking out over Bolinas Bay and south to San Francisco, fifteen miles away. The sea was flat, and the city lights shimmered on the water between here and there under the unquiet sky.

THEY FOUND AL JOHANSON'S place. They could hardly miss it—there was a high weather-beaten wooden fence with a trellis arching over it, and a gate with a sign on it that said "Johanson," with an arrow pointing at a mail slot just to the right of the gate, along with a knotted hemp rope with a tag reading "Ring Me."

Nya could see lights through the cracks in the fence.

"It's me he's expecting," Nya said. "Let me ring the bell."

"Go ahead."

Nya pulled the rope. A chorus of cowbells rattled like badly-made wind chimes.

"It's not locked!" A soft gurgle chased the words from the other side. The voice sounded as if it came from inside a musty saddlebag.

Nya gave the gate a tentative push. It swung in, revealing a scraggly garden lit by thousands of white

Christmas lights. At the far end of the path, there was a little trailer, an old one, like Nya had seen Goofy towing behind his car in the cartoons.

In front of it, in a white plastic patio chair, sat a man. Bald, very old, he looked as if someone had stretched dark leather over a stack of apples. A couple other empty chairs sat near him, the three seats gathered around an industrial cable spool that was serving as a drinks table.

"Come in, come in. Have a seat."

Nya did, wearing a smile. Rachael did too, but was all frowns.

*Come on, Rachael,* Nya thought as hard as she could, *You're gonna screw this up.*

"Mister Johanson," Nya leaned across the table, extending her hand. He shook it. His grip was solid, but just barely. "Nya Thales. I called earlier."

"Yes. Excellent, now you're here, we can turn these off." He reached down under his chair, looked like he was going to tumble sideways while doing it. "First night of the Lyrids. No city lights, you can actually see them out here. Quite a show. Quite a show."

Nya heard a click, and all the lights in the yard went out. Despite the gray glow of the moon behind the clouds about three hours above the western horizon, the overgrown garden surrounded her with a darkness thicker than any she'd seen since the night she'd first met Clarke Lantham, down in Half Moon Bay.

The thought made her shiver. That had been a bad night. A lot of people died that night. A lot of people she loved.

She couldn't see many stars. Just a few at the fringes starting to peek through the gray where the trailing edge of the storm front gave way to open sky. But she watched anyway, out of politeness.

"Assuming the clouds break up like the weatherman says they will. Who's this with you?" Al said from the darkness.

"This is Rachael Oldman."

"Oh! Yes, you said. From across the street."

"That's right. She works with Clarke and me."

"Pleased to meet you. Again." he said.

Rachael nodded to him, said something that sounded like "You too," but otherwise didn't open her mouth. In the dim, Nya could see enough of her face to detect a profound discomfort, like she suddenly didn't want to be here.

Nya didn't sense anything out of the ordinary. Just an old man and a beach trailer. Nothing unusual about the old man, either. No defensiveness, or caginess. Just some curiosity, which she figured was understandable under the circumstances. She determined to steer completely clear of the bodies, or anything that hinted at them. There was no reason to upset him.

"And how is the house? You're doing renovations. No termites I hope? Hasn't started falling down?"

"No, no, nothing like that," Nya said.

"But we found something of your brother's," Rachael cut in, hard voiced. "You have a brother, right? Seymour? Master Sergeant Seymour Johanson, US Army?"

"Oh!" He sounded shocked, and a little worried. "Yes, I have a brother, but he and I haven't spoken in Lord knows how long."

"Do you know where we could find him?"

"Maybe have his address somewhere round here. What was it you came across?"

Rachael drew in the kind of breath that would have a wallop of accusations behind it when it came out, so Nya reached out and touched her knee to shut her up, then jumped in front with: "Well...Clarke's been wanting to convert the basement into a pool room..."

"A pool?" Al said. "Down there?"

"No, like with a pool table."

"Oh. That makes more sense. Can't see why anyone'd put a swimming pool indoors like that.

Would either of you young ladies like a drink? I've got lemonade, coffee, some beer..."

"Lemonade sounds perfect," Nya said, and meant it. A cold beach evening, just a hint of salt on the air from the waves at the bottom of the bluff, stars in the sky. Lemonade, with all its sour-bright-sweet, was perfect for a day like that.

"I'm fine," Rachael said, voice all flat.

Al shifted in his chair, reached down into the spool, came up with a red Solo cup and a can of club soda. He proceeded to mix the club soda with liquid from one of the pitchers that was already on the spool. "I find the sparkle makes it better. You don't mind, do you?"

"Sounds wonderful," Nya said. "Anyway, Clarke's been talking about that all year, and he's going out of town soon and we were thinking of maybe doing it for him, like for an early birthday present. So we were down there, looking around, trying to figure out what we need to do, and we found this, I don't know, concrete lock box, I guess. Maybe to keep papers in a fire? It was under the front porch in that little stud gazebo down in the basement..."

"I know the one, yeah," Al said. He handed her the Solo cup.

"Thanks. Well, inside there were some dog tags, and a rank thing..."

"Rank insignia," Rachael grumbled.

"That. And a name tag made out of army cloth. And, well, those are the things people like to have back, so we asked around the neighborhood, and Smitty said you had a brother living there for a while who was in the army, and..." She ran out of words.

"Well, I can't take it. Isn't mine. He wouldn't want me to have it anyway. But our sister, she and he are still good. I can give you her address."

"Thanks."

"So tell me more about this pool room. What y'all gonna do with that?"

Nya shrugged. "Dig out the dirt, put in a floor, I guess. Hey, you built the house, right?" She took a drink. The soda made the lemonade light, made all the lemon smell go straight up her nose. A kind of sparkle that matched the four stars she could currently spot through the cloud layer.

"My Daddy and me, yup. Smitty helped too, when that little bastard wasn't drunker than death and screamin' at his grandkids."

"Smitty?" She had trouble imagining him that way. He was such a sweet man. Maybe people got nicer the longer they lived. She didn't know—she hadn't met any old people until she moved into Clarke's spare room.

"He was a mean old cuss, back when. Mellowed

over the years. His son finally stood up to him, made him sit back on his heels."

Nya nodded. She wished something like that would have worked out with her mother. "So, we're stuck on this thing with this project. We can't figure out what we can change down there without hurting the house itself. Like, can we put a box around the furnace so it's not just this big ugly thing in the middle of the room?"

Al let out a long breath. It settled into the background, like just another sea breeze. "I don't think you're supposed to do that. They have to breathe. There's a plaque on that one, I think. Tells you how much air it needs, in cubic feet. You don't want to box it or it has trouble with carbon monoxide. The man who installed it went on and on like you never did hear."

"Shit, now you tell us," Rachael said. "What's next, we can't dig the dirt out because it'll wreck the foundation?"

Al sighed. "Actually, that's about the size of it. My Daddy and me, when we put that house together, we poured those footings like that. They don't go down more than, what, a foot below the dirt level back there, except for the laundry room. No, you'd have to re-do the whole foundation. Be cheaper to do it out in the garage building..."

"That's our office building now." Nya crammed all the disappointment she could manage into her voice. It wasn't fake. It just wasn't about the dirt. She and Rachael were already past that depth, and the footings ran deep. Nya was betting they went down a ways longer, for drainage. She'd been reading up a lot on how basements and foundations worked in advance of the project.

He was lying to them, to keep them from digging.

"Okay, then, cheaper by a long sight just to build another outbuilding. I mean, look over yonder." He pointed across the yard to a ramshackle shed that looked like it had been cobbled together from toothpicks, old shingles, and beer bottles. "It's sounder than it looks. Last guy that lived here, that was his house. I use it for storage now, but that didn't cost him more than a thousand bucks to put up—maybe a little more to wire it—but the trick is that foundation, there. It's on stilts, and then the floor joists sit on a lattice work. They call that a pier and beam, and it's dead easy, especially if you don't need a big building. Cheap, too, and they last forever. Even do well in earthquakes."

Nya was scrambling for the right question to ask him, so she tried to keep him talking to give herself time to think. "You think something like that would work for a pool room?"

"Don't see why not. In fact, that old shed at the back of the property, betcha that's big enough for a pool table."

Nya had measured. It was big enough to store a pool table, not to play pool in. "So what would happen if we dug the dirt out?"

"You'd bring the whole house down on you is what." He jumped on the end of her question, like he wanted to shut her up. "Don't take my word for it, bring an inspector in. You'll never get a permit to do that. The county won't let you. Earthquake laws."

"Why don't you talk to your brother anymore?" Rachael dropped it like a cold boulder on the drinks table.

Al shook his head. "Looks like we aren't gonna get any stars tonight. Those clouds aren't moving a bit..."

"Al." Rachael brought him to a dead stop with her tone. "Why."

"We had a fight long time ago." Al mumbled.

"Did you." She kept phrasing things as questions. But they weren't questions.

"What did you fight about?" Nya tried to get in between them. Last thing she wanted was the risk of Rachael getting in a fistfight with a seventy five year old man, and that's where this was heading in an awful hurry.

Al shook his head. "It's not important."

He reached under his chair again, tottering right, hit whatever switch was down there, and the garden lights came on again. His leathery face didn't have any kindness left in it now. He was all strain lines and false courtesy.

"I think you girls had better get a move on, before the Fairfax police start patrolling for drunks. They'll do you for nothing, just to meet quota. You wanna get back out to the freeway before..."

"What happened, Al?" Nya asked in as soothing a voice she could muster.

"That's my business, and not yours. Now get out."

"We found the bodies." Rachael said.

"What?"

"The bodies in the basement," Nya said. "We found them this morning. While we were digging out."

"You can't dig out down there! I told you..."

"Your brother killed those kids, back in sixty-seven. When he stayed with you that summer," Rachael said. Then, with dawning astonishment, "And you knew about it. That's why you won't talk. You couldn't turn him in—why? Couldn't do that to your parents? Couldn't turn on your brother? Even after he killed your own daughter and your step-kids?

So you kicked him out. And the killings stopped. And you kept the bodies hidden all those years cause you couldn't move them. Maybe, what, you didn't have anywhere else to dump them? And you didn't think anyone would dig the basement up. And you only sold the house to someone you knew wouldn't re-sell the lot to developers who'd bulldoze it all. That's it," Rachael stood up, fished her phone out of her pocket. Started poking at the screen.

"Who do you think you're calling?" Al said.

"The FBI."

Al reached forward to the table, grabbed the lemonade pitcher, and threw the lemonade all over Rachael.

She dropped her phone.

"Don't pick it up," Al said as she was gonna squat down.

"What, are you going to find a gun and shoot me?" Rachael's hand moved to the small of her back where she carried her weapon. Part of her job with Clarke, she'd gotten the permit last year after she met the qualifications.

But she didn't draw. Just moving into position.

Nya didn't want to look away. If she did, Rachael might do something stupid.

"Just don't." He took a breath, and said again: "Don't."

Al had a tone in his voice that wasn't at all what Nya expected. Not that she knew what to expect. But it didn't feel right.

She risked tearing her gaze away from Rachael.

Al's jaw was set. Both hands were in his lap, empty. He leaned forward almost to the point of pitching over onto his nose. The pulse pounded on the side of his throat, like a little elf was trying to kick its way out. His eyes stared right through Rachael.

His cheeks twitched, just a little.

His lips trembled.

And there were small, glittering streaks moving down the sides of his nose.

"Oh my god," Nya said.

Al closed his eyes. A sob punched its way out of his throat.

And Nya knew for sure. She barely whispered: "You killed them."

Tears flowed down his face like someone had just broken the levee.

Al nodded.

"That's it." Rachael squatted down to retrieve her phone.

"Don't DO THAT," Al choked. He stood up and knocked the chair over while he did, making enough of a clatter that Rachael actually did go for her gun this time.

"Sit back down, Al. You're under arrest, and you're not going anywhere till the FBI gets here."

"You're a cop?"

"Citizen's arrest."

"Don't do this, don't do this," he started swaying. Nya leapt to her feet and righted his chair, helped him down into it. He was trembling all over.

"Why shouldn't we?" Nya asked. "All those boys and girls..."

"I didn't kill them. I killed *them*."

"Them who?" Nya looked back at Rachael, still standing tall with her gun drawn, staring down at Al like she was the second coming of Dirty Harry or something. "Rachael, for Christ's sake, sit down, put the gun away. It's not like he can outrun us."

Rachael appeared to think it over for a long moment, then sat down. She stuffed the gun in her jacket pocket, where she could get to it if she needed it. Nya rolled her eyes behind her lids.

Then she turned her attention back to the old man in the chair. "Who, Al? Who did you kill? Tell us what happened."

"It was the summer I married Jenny. Seymour watched the kids while we went up to Tahoe for our honeymoon. We were supposed to be gone for a month, but then...the telegram...my Sabrina, my daughter, she went missing. Two days. Nobody could find her. Well, of course we came right back. We looked everywhere. All the places she used to ride on her bike. The schools. The gullies and construction sites, the hidden alleys behind the elementary school, everything. You wouldn't believe how many places there are in that neighborhood where a body could just get lost..."

He swallowed hard. Took a breath. Steadied himself.

"So then we got the neighbors and the kids into it. They all looked everywhere too. Every back yard, every old car. There wasn't anything anywhere. It was like...like she just never was."

"But she was," Rachael said. Some sympathy creeping into her voice, just around the edges.

"And she was just the first. Two weeks later, just when we finally gave up finding her in town, another one. A boy this time. Robbie, from down the street where that kid Teddy lives now. Same thing. He was out playing, he never came home. No word. No trace. At least with him they found his bicycle."

Nya's breath went thin.

Al looked at her. "Do you remember the World Trade Center?"

Nya shook her head. "I was only six."

"It's like they told us in the Army. Once is

happenstance. Twice is coincidence. Three times is enemy action. Well, when the first plane hit, that was an accident. When the second one hit, then it was an attack. When my Sabrina disappeared, that was a terrible thing. When Robbie vanished, that was when we knew. Oh, the police, they didn't admit it. They said the kids were playing somewhere dangerous, and getting hurt. That kind of thing happened all the time, but they would look into it anyway, because it was their job."

"Robbie..." Rachael mumbled. "That was the one with the bicycle."

Al nodded. "They found it in the alley behind the Village. By the toy store. He was the only one they even find that much from. Then it's Amy, and Quentin, and Kim, and Adam. Every week. They just keep disappearing. No matter what we did. No matter how much we keep them inside. No matter what happened, they kept on vanishing..."

He reached a trembling hand out as if for a drink, then yanked it back to the safety of his lap without grabbing anything. "Well, I thought what you thought, I says to myself 'Seymour, he's just been in 'Nam, he's maybe not right in the head from all that killing.' So I watched him, and next time one of those kids went missing, Amy it was, well, he and I, we're off in the City trying to buy some fish off the salmon ships, so I knew it wasn't him."

This time he did grab a drink. Took a long slug of whatever was in his glass. "All summer. Until...the last one...Adam...I come home early from the job site, cause of some safety problem made them shut it down to re-rig the scaffolding. I walk home, cause it was just downtown Castro Valley. And I'm walking around to the back door, by one of the basement windows..."

Drink. "And I hears this awful noise. Like a cat screaming way off in the distance. And then again. Seems like it's come from the basement. So I squat down, I look in...*they* were in there."

"Who?" Rachael said.

"Jenny's kids. Richie and Serena."

"Your stepchildren."

"Yes. But they weren't alone. They has someone else with them. Can't see who. So I sneak in the back door, down stairs, look around the corner. They got this poor kid, Adam from next door, hanging upside down naked in the back of the basement, up over the dirt. They were cutting all over him. They'd cut his stomach open. Cut his arms open. He was bleeding like I never seen bleeding before. And they were naked too, so there wouldn't be no blood on their clothes, and..." drink "and they'd put something in him. A hammer. *In* him. Like they were getting off on it. And the two of them, they were lying on the ground like that, on top of each other, next to him, while he was screaming, and they were...together and..."

"Oh my god," Rachael whispered.

Drink.

Drink.

Nya tried to breathe, found she couldn't.

Drink.

"I just...for a minute I just couldn't believe it. Then Richie looks up from what he's doing. He sees me standing there. I run in...I've got a board all of a sudden. A bit of two-by-four. I tried to save him. I tried to save him. I tried I tried I tried. But they saw me coming, and Richie tried to stab me. He misses, gets me in the leg. Wraps around and...well that's why I've got the limp. Then I'm trying to kick him off, and Serena comes in with her knife and I just...I'd been in Korea, you see. They taught us how to do with knives. I took it from her, and I just killed them both, like that. Didn't even know I was doing it till it was over. And that poor boy, Adam, he was just shaking and crying and bleeding, but there was nothing I could do for him. He died before I could get him down."

Drink.

"So I buried them. Dressed them up so their

clothes wouldn't be found. Back in that stud cage back there? That's where they'd kept the kids they took. Tied them up in there. I found piles of shit and old blankets in there, and rope. So I called Seymour down. He helped me dress them and bury them all three down there. Helped me with the police, when we called in the report about the missing...anyway, that's why we don't talk anymore."

"So where are all the other bodies, of all the other kids?" Rachael said.

"I don't know. Down there, I guess. Or maybe out back somewhere. Those kids were always digging up something or other."

"Give us just a second, Mister Johanson. Rachael?" Nya stood up, took her girlfriend's elbow, marched her off toward the gate. "What are we gonna do?"

"Please God tell me you were recording that."

"No...no I didn't have any chance. And it wasn't supposed to be asking him about anything. I didn't know. And we didn't ask anyway."

"So we just fucked up the case without documenting any of it?" Rachael hissed the kind of hiss she hissed when she was trying not to scream. "Well, fuck. Give me your phone."

"Why?"

"FBI? Hello? For fuck's sake Nya, we gotta get

out here before he makes a run for it."

"We can't do that."

"Goddammit, Nya..."

"We *can't* do that. Really. Think what it'll do to his brother, or his son—or his grandkids. Think what they'll do to him."

"Think about what *not knowing* has done to everyone else on that block. Think about justice, for Chris's sake, Nya..."

"Justice? Rachael the kids who did this are dead..."

"The sick *fucks* who did this might be dead, but that doesn't help anyone who's been holding their breath for forty years. God, more than that. They *have* to know."

Nya folded her arms over her chest, lowered her brow. She was not, she realized, a razor sharp example of jurisprudence and legal theory, but she knew one thing for sure: "I am *not* going to let you ruin his life. Or his family's."

"His life was ruined when he married that bitch with her psycho kids! You think he *sleeps* at night? That kind of secret is probably why he drinks like he does—no, really, trust me, I was his neighbor for two years, I know."

Nya opened her mouth to speak, but Rachael held out her open hand.

Then she ticked off the fingers.

"If we cover this up, we're accessories after the fact to...whatever this winds up being. We're keeping the uncertainty going for all those people. We're keeping a secret graveyard in Lantham's house, and you know *you know* he's going to get around to digging it out himself. And what if there's more in the back yard? This is the one of the biggest unsolved crimes in Bay Area *history*. We can't just let this lie. What if Lantham decides to put a pool in someday? Or a garden? Secrets like this don't keep. They *don't*. Now give me the *fucking phone*."

Nya dug in her pocket.

She handed over the phone.

A little plastic thing. Felt like it weighted three tons.

9:34 PM, Thursday

RACHAEL ACCEPTED THE PHONE from Nya. She held onto Nya's fingers, praying all the while that nothing cracked. She couldn't afford to have anything show in her face, not now.

But she didn't want to let go.

They could leave here, like Nya had said, and call nothing in. Let the police do things the police way and take the risk that they might make the same set of connections that Rachael and Nya had.

It was tempting. Maybe there was another serial killer operating in the US at that time, that had the same kind of MO, and the cops would connect it to him. Or maybe the FBI Behavioral Psychologists would classify it as the work of a previously-undocumented and currently unfindable serial killer. The ultimate cold case that would never warm up again. The kind that criminology students would study when the next round of textbooks came out.

Maybe.

It was, she knew, the kind of lying that made for a good cop. Or a good PI. You figure out what the truth is, and when the truth means a killer gets away with it, or the good guys suffer, you fudge a little. You smear the ink on your reports, you use ambiguous language, and one way or another you make sure the bad guy goes away.

That's how police departments had always operated. The people that were bad for society, they got handed over to the DA, even on weak cases. And the people who weren't? Well, they walked, or got slapped on the wrists. Or they endured a little scandal. But prison? Lethal injection? Not if any cop worth his salt could help it.

The right people got off.

The right fucking people.

Because God knows the *right people* are easy to spot. You can *always* tell who they are. And the world would be perfect, if only you could make sure that the *right people* always came out on top.

Always the right fucking people.

Well, Rachael knew who deserved to win. And she knew who deserved to lose. And she knew that if racist cops and bent judges and self-righteous guardians of culture and insular fucking college professors didn't qualify to be the queens of the universe, then she sure as shit didn't either. Especially not today. Not in a case like this. Not with so much blood on the ground. This wasn't shoplifting. This wasn't even a murder. This was the kind of case where there was no such thing as the "right call." The kind of case that would turn into law.

It was the kind of case where there had been too many secrets, for too long.

And it was time for the secrets to come out.

But she didn't know how to explain all that to Nya. She didn't know how to tell her that people would suffer no matter what the two of them did, or who they called. All that damage was done the moment they decided to dig in the basement.

Once that happened, the rest of it would happen one way or the other. Old ghosts would have come back to haunt everyone, and, sooner or later, someone would have found Al, and his brother, and learned the truth.

The world worked like that, sometimes.

Sometimes, no matter what you did, you eventually had no good choices left.

"I'm sorry," Rachael said. And she squeezed Nya's hand. And hoped Nya could forgive her.

Then Rachael took the phone.

"I'm going to go make sure he's okay," Nya said.

"This could take a while. I'll come back in when I'm done."

Nya nodded. She turned her back on Rachael and strode slowly back to where Al was sitting. Heavy feet. Like she was walking through deep mud.

Rachael looked away. She stepped out through the gate, and shuffled along the gravel-paved road until she was out of earshot. Then she called information.

"San Francisco FBI. I need the twenty-four hour line."

*UNBURDEN YOURSELF.* Nya'd heard that all her life.

From her parents. From the people in church.

*Confession is good for the soul.*

*God loves the contrite spirit.*

One way or another, they all added up to the same thing. You unbury your deep shame. You tell your secrets. You trust somebody. And it lightens the load. It soothes your grief. It gladdens your heart.

Once upon a time, Nya might have thought so too. Her secrets never hid very far away. Even her worst memories were centered around people who she truly loved, and she'd never been willing to sacrifice that love in order to forget the pain it brought.

But she wasn't normal. She knew it. For other people, secrets got buried. Like fish in a flower bed. They made a kind of fertilizer. Lives grew in those flowerbeds. Dig them up, and the lives wilted. Or shattered.

Like Al was now. Everything that made him Al seemed to have left him. He slumped in his seat, his cheeks soaking, his nose red and running. He stared at the wooden spool, as if he could find the meaning of life in the patina on the rivets.

Nya laid her hand on his left arm. "It's all right, Al. It really is. You didn't have a choice. You did the right thing."

He patted her hand, shook his head. "How old are you?"

"Twenty-one. Just last month."

He took her hand in his. Set it back on her lap. "That's what I thought."

"What's that supposed to mean?"

He sniffed. Adjusted his posture. "It means that I appreciate it. But I don't need it."

"Al..."

"No. Don't say anything more. Just leave me alone. Call whoever you need to." He blinked a few more times. Then he wiped his face with the heels of his hands. He looked at her with clear eyes. "Please, young lady. Sincerely. Go home. Enjoy it. Get the bodies out of there, and make it a living place. If you want to help me, that's all I ask."

Nya tried to read him. He looked calm. Calmer than she would have believed.

Maybe she'd been wrong. Maybe confession *really* was good for the soul.

Nya nodded.

She stood up.

"I'm sorry." she said.

"Things come out," he said, with a tone that sounded like he was trying to make her feel better. "Jenny's dead. She'll never have to know. God grants his small mercies. They get you by."

He smiled a small, crooked smile. "You go on now. Take her phone. Tell her I'm sorry I ruined it."


RACHAEL STOOD ON THE edge of a crumbling roadway—the ground beneath had been eaten away by the sea, sometime recently enough that the city, if there was a city up here, hadn't gotten around to fixing it yet—and hung up the phone.

The Bolinas Sheriff's department was coming. They'd be here any minute. They would take her statement and make an investigation, and decide whether or not to take Al in as a suspect, or a material witness, or whether to just leave him alone.

All by the book.

Just like it should be.

The ocean stretched flat and calm all the way to the San Francisco coast line. Fifteen open miles.

Miles as empty as solving a serial killing. Cold, too.

"Twatmonster?" Nya's footsteps crossed from gravel to pavement a little ways behind her.

"Monkeybrain. Everything okay?"

"He seemed to be." Her voice was all shrugs.

"Fed'll be here in a few minutes." Rachael wrapped her arms around herself. "We'll need to stay and give statements."

"Are you okay?" Nya's arm slid around Rachael's waist.

Rachael shrugged. "Not really."

"It didn't work, did it?"

Rachael shook her head. "I don't know what's next."

Nya squeezed her. Kissed her shoulder. "Yeah, you do."

Rachael sighed. Nya meant Lantham. Rachael had been avoiding him, one way or another, for months, because she didn't want to tell him how she felt about him. She wasn't sure if she was more afraid he'd say he didn't feel the same way, or that he'd say that he did. Because either way, it would change everything in her life, and there'd been too much change. You were supposed to get out on your own, get into a career, and then do your thing. Maybe change careers when you got bored or when the market changed. But you weren't supposed to have to deal with everything in your life going sideways once or twice a year...were you?

Maybe not. Maybe that was just the kind of shit they sold to you in high school to keep you from skipping class. Maybe real life was all tumult, and the whole point of it was to see how long you could survive it.

Maybe. But if it was, then she had to find some way to make it work for her. She didn't do chaos well, and she sure as hell didn't like hopeless situations.

"I don't think so. It's hopeless."

"No it's not," Nya said. "You know how I know things, right?"

"Yeah."

"Then trust me."

And there it was. If she couldn't trust Nya, after all this time, who could she trust?

"Okay."

# 4:00 AM, Friday

THE COPS ARRIVED RIGHT AFTER that. They took statements. They held everyone there until the Feds showed up.

Special Agent In Charge Ronald Rivers took one look at Nya and Rachael and said "Figures," then got on with his job without so much as a hello.

There was another round of questions, and there was the offloading of the recordings to the laptop in the big black Suburban.

Then there was the emergency microwave egg roll run at the 7-11 in Fairfax once Rachael and Nya finally got released and started heading home. They rolled in the driveway an hour later.

Tomorrow the FBI would be at Lantham's house with the full excavation team.

"Look at it this way," Rachael said to Nya, who was not looking forward to having her home infested with strangers for the next several days, "They're going to do a *lot* of digging for us."

"After all that death, that old basement needs something living in it." Nya smiled. "Do you want to stay?"

"While that graveyard's down there?" Rachael snorted. "No thank you. Anyway...I need the time. Got some thinking to do."

Nya kissed her. Told her to be sure to get sleep. That tomorrow was going to be a big day. Tonight, Rachael didn't mind being mother-henned a little bit. It helped the world feel normal, when the day had been anything but.

The early morning chill had a touch of fog rising. It had chased the rain in from the coast, thin enough to make everything on Santa Maria feel blurry. Like there were ghosts hanging around, just waiting to step out and tell you their stories.

But they didn't step out for Rachael. Not now that she knew them all.

She crossed the road, headed the two buildings south to her condo complex, let herself in, sat on the crocheted green-and-white afghan that her grandmother had made her for her twelfth birthday, that she used as a couch blanket.

Her Lantham-customized high-power Emperor Linux laptop was on the glass-topped coffee table. She opened it, woke it up, opened up Skype.

She figured that, with the way Lantham basically

had his phone implanted in his brain, he'd be logged into Skype and waiting for someone—anyone—to call him and save him from the cruel fate that was vacation, she had a good chance of him picking up.

And she knew that if she waited till morning, she'd chicken out. Or make the call all business, warning him about the feds tearing his house apart and asking if there was anything he needed her to hide.

She had to do that, too, of course. But there was something else she needed to tell him first.

Rachael clicked on the green button next to Lantham's name.

Skype hummed its dumb little tune.

"Rache?" Lantham's voice. She could hear some kind of engine in the background.

"Yeah, Lantham, it's me."

"What's wrong?"

"Got somewhere private we can hop on video? There's...something we need to talk about."

The End
*Clarke Lantham will return*

# Acknowledgments

AS WITH ANY BOOK, long or short, thanks are do to the people who made it possible.

Many of them will never read this book. The neighborhood characters in this book are all tributes to the surrogate grandparents and neighbors I grew up around—mixed up, fictionalized, and definitely not-recognizable to anyone but me, they are nevertheless the mental and social furniture of my childhood, and as comfortable and dearly missed to me as any wonderful old sofa-and-blanket combination that comforted the kid-you-once-were during illnesses, tragedies, and losses.

Elizabeth Gibson, Sue Biaman, and Kitty NicIaian all lent their eagle eyes to the process—tracking down continuity errors, zapping copy editing problems, complaining about unclear sentences, and attempting valiantly (and sometimes successfully) to convince me to dial back my abusive relationship with the English language.

And, of course, Kitty NicIaian, as the publisher at AWP as well as my editor, did an amazing job seeing the book put together, packaged well, and delivered with style into your Lantham-starved fingers.

Finally, and in this case, most importantly, major thanks for this one goes to Kristine Kathryn Rusch. Originally written as a short story for one of her craft workshops, she knocked this back to me saying "this needs to be longer" and listing a number of plot problems—all caused by shortcuts I was taking to fit the idea to length. And, of course, doing it right took it well out of short story territory and into my favorite length for a Lantham story, the short novel.

Kris, if you're reading this, thanks loads. This book would not be what it is without you.

And, for the rest of you, if you want someone to blame...

...never mind. I value my life too much. It's all my fault. Send hate mail my way.

# Author's Note

Since I've said it in public enough times that it's not exactly a secret anymore, I might as well admit it here: I grew up in Lantham's house.

I don't mean he was my father. Lantham and my father couldn't be father apart in most ways—their capacity for violence, their approach to religion, their language. They both share a love of fast cars and bad puns, but they're otherwise not much alike.

I mean that, in these books, Lantham owns the house I grew up in. One of my longtime dreams was to buy it back when I got old enough and rich enough, and when it became clear that such was not compatible with my other goals in life, I had Lantham buy it instead.

And it was a great house to grow up in, with its multiple detached buildings, its plethora of plum trees, its vast expanses of virgin grass just aching to be dug up and turned into a stage for trench warfare between opposing camps of water-balloon-wielding nine-year-olds—I'm not admitting it actually happened, but I will say that it's amazing how fast you can turn a spade when you realize that there's a big hole to fill in and your Dad is only a half-hour away—and its glorious, terrifying basement.

There were a lot of secrets in that basement.

There was an old concrete firebox with fragments of blueprints and patches from an army uniform. There were holes hidden beneath, where previous residents had buried trash during hard times when they couldn't afford garbage service. My brothers and I unearthed vintage toys (which we played with and destroyed, having no conception of their value), clothes from the 1950s, old discarded soup cans and beer cans, even the occasional chicken bone and tool.

We had grand dreams, my three brothers and I, of digging out the entire basement so we'd have room to build a pool table. And we thought that there might be treasure buried down there, maybe from an old bank robbery, buried alongside the bodies of the partners who got double-crossed.

There weren't any neighborhood legends about such things, it just seemed to us that that's how things worked. We felt we were well-qualified on this account, having studied archeology extensively in the school of Indiana Jones, not to mention our nuanced and complete understanding of the criminal mind drawn from careful analysis of dozens upon dozens of Hardy Boys books.

Alas for my younger self, there was no treasure that we could find (except those toys whose value we didn't appreciate). And, despite all our searching, we never did find any bodies in the basement, despite long winter rainstorms spent in the dirt, with flashlights and shovels, in the fervent and inexhaustible hope of wealth and fame.

But we did learn a lot about the history of that neighborhood. And the old men and women that had lived there since it was first built never lacked for stories, and never got offended when they caught us hunting for treasure in their abandoned sheds, playing hide and seek in their bushes, or setting up bicycle ramps on their sidewalks or archery ranges on the other side of their back fence.

The neighborhood hasn't changed a lot since then, at least not as far as the buildings are concerned. But the people that connected it to its beginnings are all long dead.

Except, perhaps, a little bit, in the pages of this book.


—J. Daniel Sawyer
March 2016
Lincoln City, OR

# Also by J. Daniel Sawyer

**The Kabrakan Ascendency**
The Orinthal Deception
The Hartman Gambit
The Reeves Directive

**The Clarke Lantham Mysteries**
And Then She Was Gone
A Ghostly Christmas Present
Smoke Rings
Silent Victor
He Ain't Heavy
In The Cloud
Blood and Weeds
Bodies In The Basement

**Suave Rob's Awesome Adventures**
Suave Rob's Double-X Derring-Do
Suave Rob's Rough-n-Ready Rugrat Rescue

**Standalone Works**
Down From Ten
The Resurrection Junket
Ideas, Inc.

**Collections**
Sculpting God: Bedtime Stories for Adults
Frock Coat Dreams: Romances, Nightmares, and Fancies from the Steampunk Fringe

*Nonfiction*

**The Every Day Novelist**
Business 101
The Every Day Novelist

**Writer's Guides**
Science Fiction Weaponry: A Guide for Writers (with Mary Mason)
Throwing Lead: A Writer's Guide to Firearms and the People Who Use Them (with Mary Mason)
Making Tracks: A Writer's Guide to Audiobooks and How to Produce Them

# About the Author

With the advent of his hard-boiled *Clarke Lantham Mysteries*, J. Daniel Sawyer's abusive behavior toward the English language finally landed him in serious trouble, and he now spends his days and nights chained to a desk in a vain attempt to write his way out of the loony bin. Unfortunately, his attempts have yielded further entries in his sci-fi thriller series *The Antithesis Progression*, the cabin fever comedy *Down From Ten*, and significant alterations in his medication. On the rare occasion that he slips his bonds, he escapes to the wilds of the San Francisco back country where he devotes his energies to running afoul of local traffic ordinances in his never-ending pursuit of the ultimate driving road.

*Should you be so inclined, you can communicate with this shady character, as well as find stories, podcasts, articles, and other literary abominations at http://www.jdsawyer.net*

www.ingramcontent.com/pod-product-compliance
Lightning Source LLC
Chambersburg PA
CBHW020253150626
46552CB00020B/844